A Giraffe Did One

Illustrated by
Tatjana Mai-Wyss

By Jerry Pallotta

Published by Sleeping Bear Press

To Coco, Louisa, Nora, and Joe, the little animals in my life.
— Tatjana

To Joey IV, Madeline, Hannah, and Carter.
— Jerry

Text Copyright © 2012 Jerry Pallotta
Illustration Copyright © 2012 Tatjana Mai-Wyss

Sleeping Bear Press™

315 East Eisenhower Parkway, Suite 200
Ann Arbor, MI 48108
www.sleepingbearpress.com

© 2012 Sleeping Bear Press is an imprint of Gale, a part of Cengage Learning.
10 9 8 7 6 5 4 3 2 1
Library of Congress Cataloging-in-Publication Data
Pallotta, Jerry. A giraffe did one / by Jerry Pallotta ; illustrated by Tatjana Mai-Wyss.
p. cm.
ISBN 978-1-58536-641-5
1. Human body--Juvenile humor. 2. Animals--Juvenile humor. I. Mai-Wyss, Tatjana, 1972- II. Title.
PN6231.H763P35 2011
818'.602--
2011029115

Printed by China Translation & Printing Services Limited,
Guangdong Province, China. 1st printing. 11 / 2011

An ant did one, but no one could hear it.

A worm did one, but it was underground.

A mouse did it.
It was barely a sound.

A flock of birds flew by. OK, who did it?

We'll never know which one it was.

A squirrel did one.
Luckily, no one was around.

A skunk did one. It wasn't as bad as usual.

A turtle did one. It made a little bubble.

When a pig did it,
it was nothing but trouble.

The fox was sneaky when she did it.

The frog was slimy when he did it.

A wolf did one while howling at the night sky.

A monkey did one,
and started laughing,
but why?

A dolphin did one just as it splashed.

A manatee did one as a wave crashed.

A snake did one near the ground.

A buzzard did one up high while flying around.

A penguin did one in the icy chill.

A black bear did it while climbing a hill.

A spider did one while spinning silk.

A cow did one while giving milk.

It's sad! A flower can't do one.

And a tree can't do one either.

A herd of elk
do it while running.

A pride of lions do it while sunning.

A giraffe did one
up high with a shake.

When the elephant does it, watch out! It sounds like an EARTHQUAKE!

A whale did one! It was the biggest in the history of the world.

Then I did one, too! My mom said,
"Please say,
EXCUSE ME!"